Here We Go Round the Mulberry Bush

Sophie Fatus

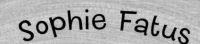

Here we go round the mulberry bush,
the mulberry bush, the mulberry bush.

Here we go round the mulberry bush,
early in the morning.

This is the way we jump out of bed,
jump out of bed, jump out of bed.

This is the way we jump out of bed,
early in the morning.

This is the way we wash ourselves,
wash ourselves, wash ourselves.

This is the way we wash ourselves,
early in the morning.

This is the way we brush our teeth,
brush our teeth, brush our teeth.

This is the way we brush our teeth,
early in the morning.

This is the way we comb our hair,
comb our hair, comb our hair.

This is the way we comb our hair,
early in the morning.

This is the way we put on our clothes,
put on our clothes, put on our clothes.

This is the way we put on our clothes,
early in the morning.

This is the way we eat our food,
eat our food, eat our food.

This is the way we eat our food,
early in the morning.

This is the way we clean our bowls,
clean our bowls, clean our bowls.

This is the way we clean our bowls
early in the morning.

This is the way we go to school,
go to school, go to school.

This is the way we go to school,
early in the morning.

This is the way we wave good-bye,
wave good-bye, wave good-bye.

This the way we wave good-bye,

good-bye, khanbiafo, namaste, joi gin

early in the morning!

Here We Go Round the Mulberry Bush

Here we go round the mul-ber-ry bush, the mul-ber-ry bush, the

mul-ber-ry bush. Here we go round the mul-ber-ry bush, ear-ly in the mor-ning.

This is the way we jump out of bed . . .

This is the way we wash ourselves . . .

This is the way we brush our teeth . . .

This is the way we comb our hair . . .

This is the way we put on our clothes . . .

This is the way we eat our food . . .

This is the way we clean our bowls . . .

This is the way we go to school . . .

This is the way we wave good-bye . . .

Early in the morning!

The Song

"Here We Go Round the Mulberry Bush" is a traditional song that has been around for hundreds of years. There are lots of stories about where it came from.

In some versions of the story, a mulberry bush is said to keep people safe. Joining hands in a circle and dancing to the right keeps evil fairies away. In other versions, the game was created by a washerwoman, so her children could play nearby while she worked. She made up a rhyme and dance about the mulberry bush in her yard. In the Celtic tradition, during country weddings, known as *rush weddings*, it was common to dance around a mulberry bush.

Whichever the story, a fun fact is that mulberries grow on trees, not bushes! The trees have heart-shaped leaves and grow red fruit on their branches.

The Dance

There is a fun dancing game that goes along with this song. Everyone holds hands and starts to sing and dance or skip around in a circle. For each verse, everyone stops to do what the song says. When you sing this verse:

"This is the way we brush our teeth, brush our teeth, brush our teeth. This is the way we brush our teeth, early in the morning."

. . . you pretend that you are brushing your teeth. You can even make up your own verses as you go along!

For my precious friend Dona — S. F.

Barefoot Books
124 Walcot Street
Bath BA1 5BG, UK

Barefoot Books
2067 Massachusetts Ave
Cambridge, MA 02140, USA

First published in Great Britain by Barefoot Books, Ltd and in
the United States of America by Barefoot Books, Inc in 2007
This paperback edition published in 2008
All rights reserved. No part of this book may be reproduced in any form
or by any means, electronic or mechanical, including photocopying,
recording or by any information storage and retrieval system,
without permission in writing from the publisher

Graphic design by Louise Millar, London
Reproduction by Grafiscan, Verona
Printed and bound in Singapore by Tien Wah Press Pte Ltd

The Library of Congress cataloged the hardcover edition as follows:
Fatus, Sophie.
   Here we go round the mulberry bush / Sophie Fatus.
      p. cm.
   Summary: Presents ten verses of the popular song, with illustrations
of children from different cultures as they get ready for school.
   ISBN-13: 978-1-84686-035-5 (hardcover : alk. paper)
   1. Children's songs, English--United States--Texts.   [1. Morning
--Songs and music. 2. Songs.]   I. Title.
PZ8.3.F2345Her 2007
782.42--dc22
[E]

                              2006025656

British Cataloguing-in-Publication Data:
a catalogue record for this book is available from the British Library

                    1 3 5 7 9 8 6 4 2